If I Were
A Tree

written & illustrated by

Dar Hosta

BROWN DOG
books

Brown Dog Books
Flemington, New Jersey

First Edition, Copyright © 2007 by Dar Hosta
ISBN-10: 0-9721967-3-0, ISBN-13: 978-0-9721967-3-4
Library of Congress Control Number: 2006910541

Published by Brown Dog Books
PO Box 2196, Flemington, NJ 08822
www.browndogbooks.com

Hello Friends,

What is it that makes us love a tree?

For thousands of years, trees have
inspired poets, writers, musicians, and
artists and have been featured in the
folklore, mythology, and storytelling
of every culture on Earth. Trees are
a symbol of strength and grace,
of permanence and the cycles of
change, and of community and
solitude. A tree may represent family,
marriage, knowledge, life, and love.
Trees can be a part of our childhood

To help in the reduction of greenhouse gases, and to contribute to the environmental effort to save millions of trees and billions of gallons of water, this book was printed on *OK Matt Kote Green 100*, 100% recycled paper.

The illustrations were created with collage. The type is Century Gothic. Book design by Dar Hosta.

Printed in China

memories, often growing up along with us. Trees bring life into our urban settings, and become the natural landmarks of our own personal piece of the planet. Their steadfastness and longevity make them the silent witnesses to an ever-changing world.

This book is a celebration of trees and of the comfort and joy that this simple, natural image brings to us all

Other books by Dar Hosta

I Love The Night

I Love The Alphabet

Mavis & Her Marvelous Mooncakes

You can find out more about Dar Hosta at

www.darhosta.com

This book is dedicated to my
courageously courageous Sister...

If I were a tree, Bāadi, I would
grow the cure.

Oh, how would it be

if you were a tree?

If I were a tree, my favorite colors would be

green...

and yellow...

and orange...

and red.

If I were a tree,

I would have conversations with

the sky...

and the sun...

and the stars...

and the moon.

If I were a tree,

I would wave to you

whenever

the wind blows.

How would it be

if you were a tree?

If I were a tree,

I would bring you

a burst of blossoms

in the springtime.

If I were a tree, I would give you

cool shade in the summer.

If I were a tree,

I would show you

colorful leaves

in the fall.

If I were a tree, I would be quiet...

and still...

and patient

through winter's chill.

And, I would let the snowflakes

rest on my branches.

So, how would it be if you were a tree?

If I were a tree,

I would be a pear tree

and bear a season's

golden treasure.

I would be a lemon tree

and life would be forever sweet.

I would be

an apple tree

so that you

could make a pie.

If you were a tree,

what kind of tree

would you be?

I would be

a cherry tree

just to make

you cheery.

I would be

a city tree

and remind you

of the whispers

of leaves.

I would be

a happy tree,

and a friend

to all the creatures

of the Earth.

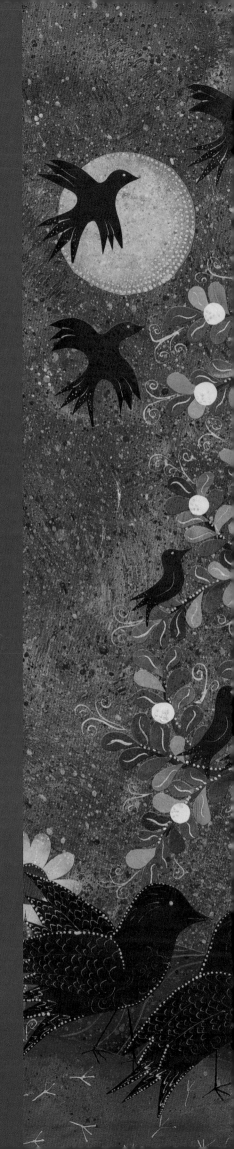

If I were a tree,

my branches

would always be

full of song,

and I would cradle

a nest for you

to come home to.

Oh yes, if I could not be me

it would be nice to be a tree.

All of the **LEAVES** together make up the **CROWN**.

Small **BRANCHES** are called **TWIGS**.

The **BRANCHES** support the **LEAVES**.

The **TRUNK** supports the **BRANCHES**.

The **BARK** protects the tree from injury.

The **HEARTWOOD** gives the tree its strength.

The **SAPWOOD** carries sap from the **ROOTS** to the **LEAVES**.

The **ROOTS** hold the tree in the ground and take up water and nutrients from the soil.

LEAVES are green because they contain a green pigment called **CHLOROPHYLL**.

Trees have been on Earth for over 370 million years, and they live longer than any other organism on the planet.

There are more than 80,000 different species of trees.

Trees absorb carbon dioxide from the atmosphere and replace it with oxygen.

With the help of the sun, the **LEAVES** make all the food a tree needs.

This process is called **PHOTOSYNTHESIS**.

Forests reduce soil erosion, regulate water flow, and help control the effects of flooding.

Trees grow everywhere on Earth, from the chill of the Arctic Circle to the heat of the Equator.

Trees grow fruit, nuts, and flowers.

To Be A Tree...

Grow strong and reach for the sky,

send out roots and make yourself a place,

withstand the winds of all seasons,

and always welcome those

who sing with joy.

~Dar Hosta

Dar Hosta makes her home in central New Jersey, where she lives with her husband, her two sons, and two big brown dogs. There are many trees that grow around her house, and her favorite is a majestic oak tree that stands nearly four stories tall. *If I Were A Tree* is her fourth picture book for children.

Photograph by Lou Hosta